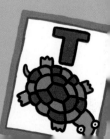

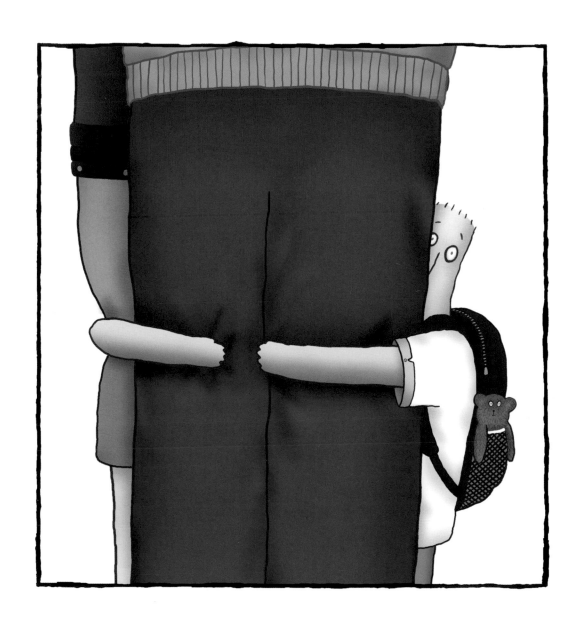

For great teachers everywhere,
especially my sister,
Ellen.

A FEIWEL AND FRIENDS BOOK
An Imprint of Macmillan

Library of Congress Cataloging-in-Publication Data Available

ISBN-13: 978-0-312-36798-5
ISBN-10: 0-312-36798-8

First Edition: July 2008

1   3   5   7   9   10   8   6   4   2

The text type is set in 32-point Hank.

Feiwel and Friends logo designed by Filomena Tuosto

Book design by Rich Deas

www.feiwelandfriends.com

JAKE

STARTS SCHOOL

By Michael Wright

FEIWEL AND FRIENDS
NEW YORK

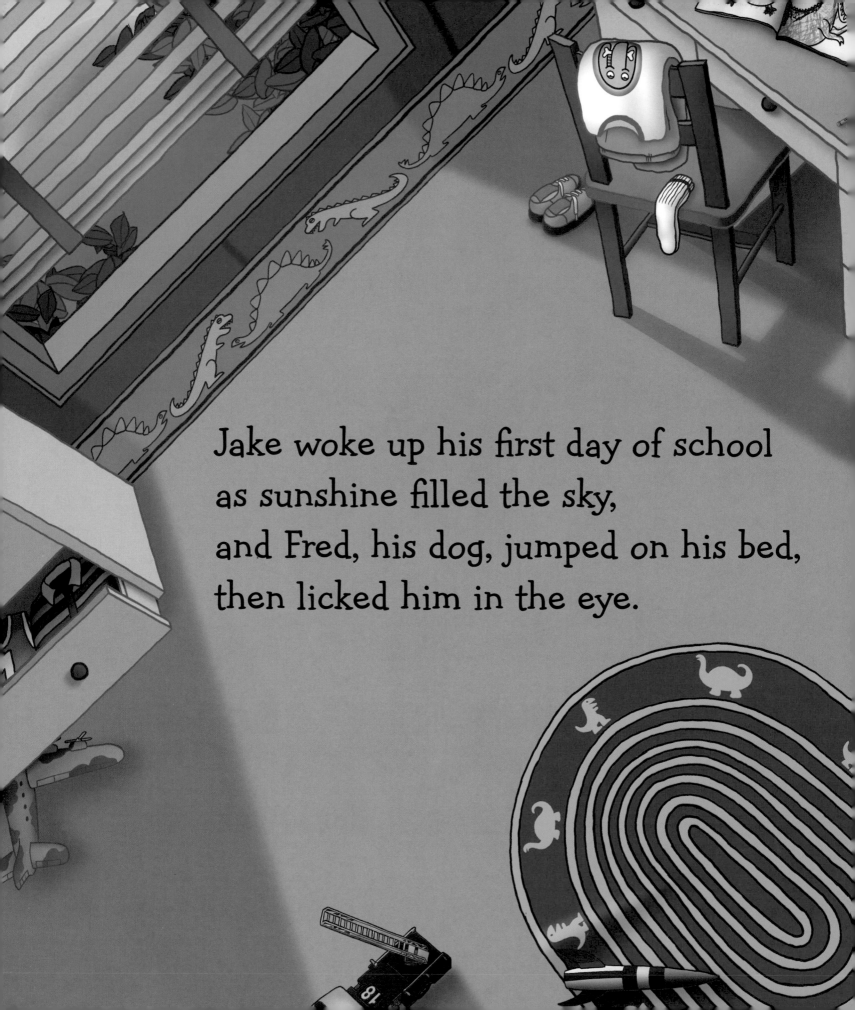

Jake woke up his first day of school
as sunshine filled the sky,
and Fred, his dog, jumped on his bed,
then licked him in the eye.

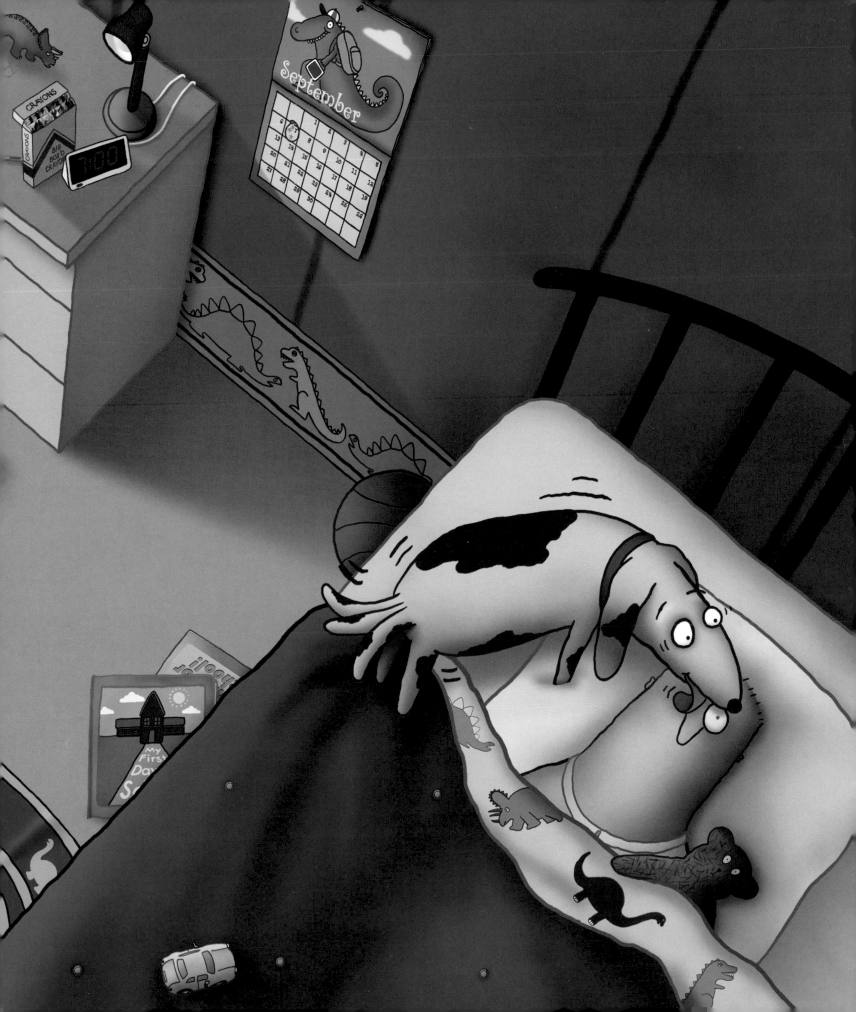

Jake brushed
his teeth,
he combed his hair,
he wore his
favorite shirt.

And packed inside his lunch box were two cookies for dessert.

When Mom and Dad called,
"Time to go!"
they drove off in the van,
to Jake's first fun-filled day of schoo

As they arrived, Jake was surprised to see so many kids.

Some of them he'd seen before,
but most he never did.

Then there it was, Room Number 1,
where Jake would join his class.
It looked *so* big, he felt *so* small,
he passed a little gas.

Just then, the door swung open and
a red-haired lady said…

Jake screamed, and then
he fled.

He grabbed his parents at the knees
and would not let them go.
They told him "Please, we have to leave,"
but all he'd say was "NO!"

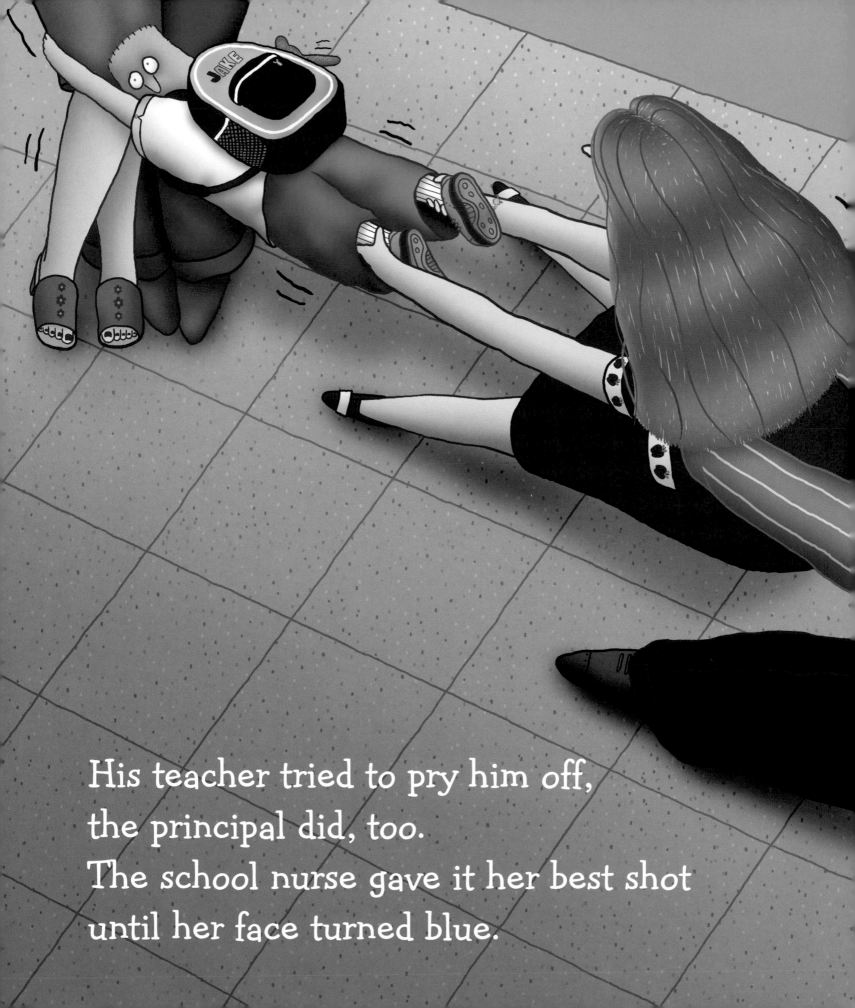

His teacher tried to pry him off,
the principal did, too.
The school nurse gave it her best shot
until her face turned blue.

"There is no choice," his teacher's voice
said to the clumping mass.
"It's looking like the three of you
will have to come to class."

They walked into the room as one
and tried to be discreet.
But that's not easy when you've got
three people in a seat.

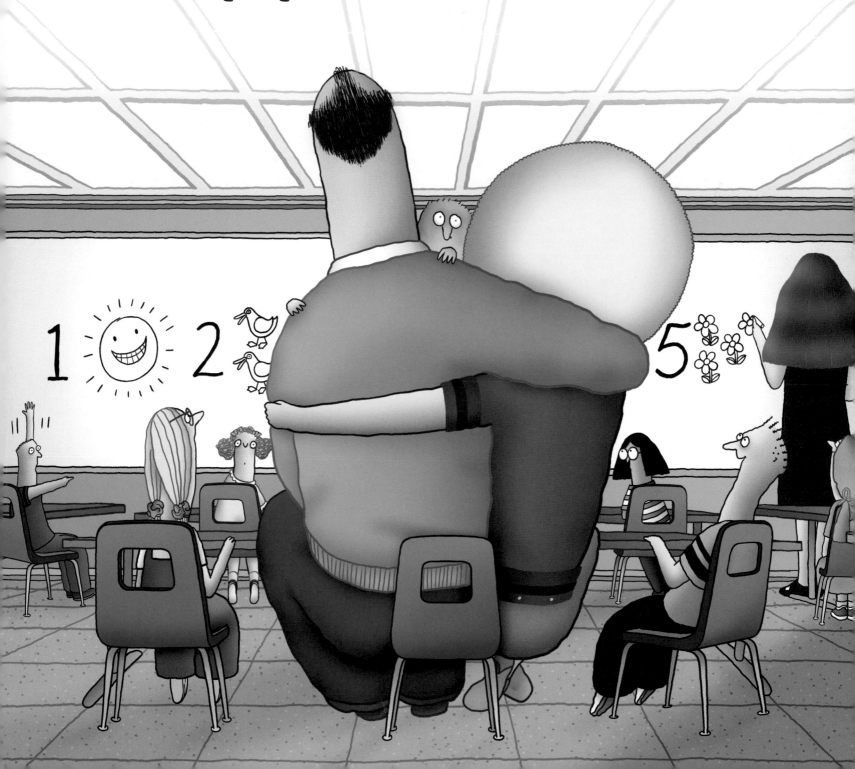

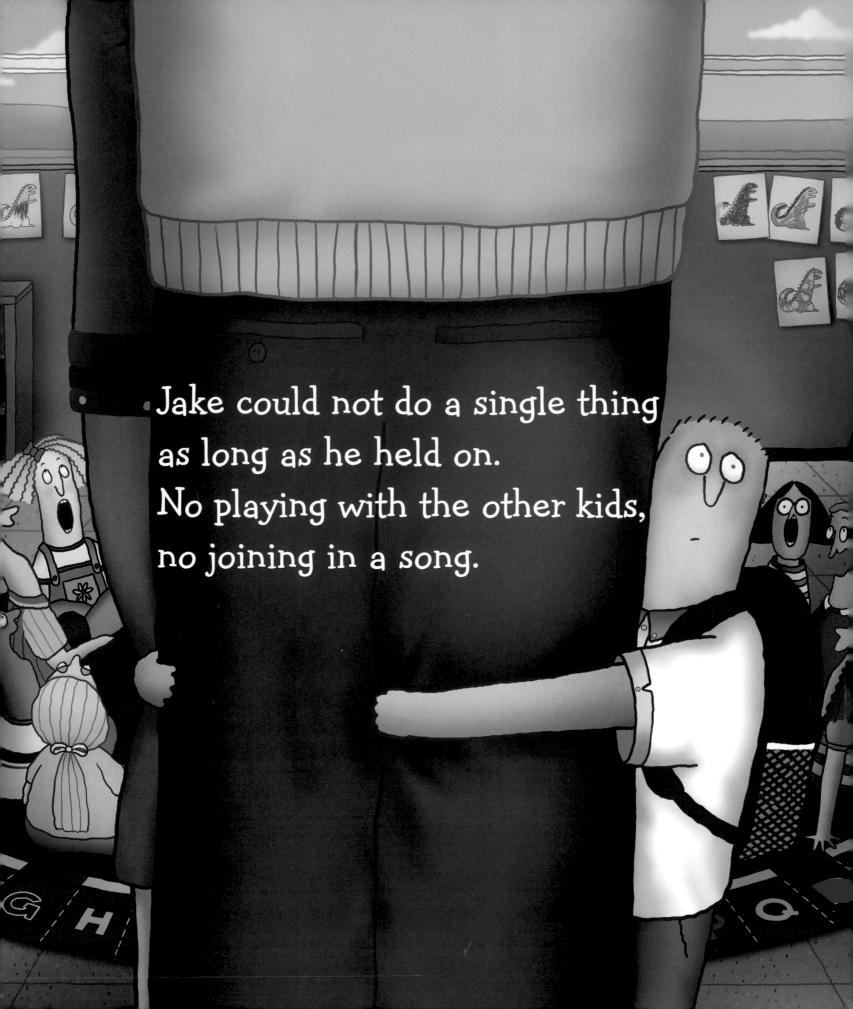

Jake could not do a single thing
as long as he held on.
No playing with the other kids,
no joining in a song.

Finger painting was no fun
without a hand or two.
His clay would stay a blob all day,
he could not squirt the glue.

They tried to take a seesaw ride
but didn't have much fun.

It's just no good when one side's light
and the other weighs a ton.

The tricycles were terrible,

so was the jungle gym.

He could not take
a bathroom break.
He had to hold it in.

He could not feed the classroom pets,
the turtle or the bird.
There was no way to make a friend.
He didn't speak a word.

His teacher finally told the class
that soon the bell would ring
and school would let out for the day.
But there was
"One more thing....

I'd like
to read a story before
our day is through.
So everybody take your place, and
I will read to you.

She turned and reached
up on the shelf
and found
one special book.

This one's about
a dog named Fred.
Why don't we take
a look?

Then from the back part of the room, there came a tiny sound.

His teacher grinned and asked,

That's when Jake let his parents go,
and they felt some relief.
It'd been a while since they had
some feeling in their feet.

With every page, Jake loosened up,
and saw from where he stood,
the whole class sat and smiled at him.
And inside, he felt good.

And when the closing bell rang out,
Jake looked to Mrs. Moore.
And gave her his last cookie
as he walked right out the door.

This whole first year with Mrs. Moore
has been a lot of fun.
Jake's special place to learn and grow
is classroom Number 1.